This book is set in English and in Cree.

There are several dialects of Cree — in this book we are using the n-dialect, also known as Swampy Cree from the Cumberland House area. *Wild Berries* is available as *Pakwa che Menisu* ᐸᐠᐘ ᒋ ᒥᓂᓱ, which is written in the n-dialect Cree, from the Cross Lake, Norway House area, and also published by Simply Read Books. More information about the Cree language and a pronunciation guide are available at the end of this book.

JULIE FLETT

Simply Read Books

Published in 2013 by Simply Read Books
www.simplyreadbooks.com

Library and Archives Canada Cataloguing in Publication
Flett, Julie
Wild berries / written and illustrated by Julie Flett.
ISBN 978-1-897476-89-5
I. Title.
PS8611.L484W54 2012 jC813'.6 C2011-907052-9

We gratefully acknowledge for their financial support of our publishing program the Canada Council for the Arts, the BC Arts Council, and the Government of Canada through the Canada Book Fund (CBF).

Book design by Robin Mitchell Cranfield for hundreds & thousands

Typeset in Californian FB by Frederic Goudy, digitized by Carol Twombly and revised for Font Bureau by David Berlow and in Poetica by Robert Slimbach

Manufactured in Malaysia

10 9 8 7 6 5 4 3 2 1

WILD BERRIES
PIKACI-MINISA

julie flett

When Clarence was little, his grandma carried him on her back through the woods to the clearing to pick

wild berries
pikaci-mīnisa.

Grandma carried a bucket and sang.

Now Clarence carries his own bucket
and walks behind his

grandma
ōkoma.

They sing together.

Blueberries dot the clearing.

Grandma checks for

bears

maskwak.

They pick the plumpest berries they can find and drop them into their

buckets
otaskīkowāwa.

Tup, tup.

Grandma likes sweet

blueberries
ininimina,

soft blueberries, juicy blueberries. Clarence likes big blueberries, sour blueberries, blueberries that go POP in his mouth.

Clarence and his grandma pick blueberries for a

long time
konēsk.

They eat

so many
mīcēt

berries that their lips turn purple.

An *ant*

ēnik crawls up Clarence's leg.

Tch, tch. It tickles.

A *spider*
kōkom-mināk̄ēsīs makes its web.

Sh, sh.

A *fox*
mākēsīs sneaks by.

Rustle, rustle.

When the buckets are full, Clarence lays a handful of berries on a leaf for the

birds
pinēsīsak

and the other animals of the woods.

They say

thank you

nanāskomowak.

Clarence and his grandma walk back through the

woods
sakāk

with their buckets full of berries.

The birds

sing

nikamo

in the clearing.

pronunciation guide

THE CREE LANGUAGE is a part of the Algonquian language family. There are several dialects of Cree: Plains Cree "y" dialect, Woodlands Cree "th" dialect, Swampy Cree "n" dialect, Moose Cree "l" dialect, and Atikamêk Cree "r" dialect. There is considerable diversity between dialects, including differences in pronunciation, vocabulary, and grammar. From region to region, there are also often differences within the same dialect. The words in this version of *Wild Berries, Pikaci-Mīnisa* are all in the n-dialect, which is also known as Swampy Cree, or Nēhinawēwin, from the Cumberland House area. Simply Read Books has produced another version of this book, *Pakwa che Menisu*, written entirely in the n-dialect, which is from the Cross Lake, Norway House area.

The Nēhinawēwin, or Swampy Cree, words you see in this book are written using the Roman alphabet. Roman orthography is an orthographic tool used to record and represent the sounds of the languages phonetically. The Cumberland House region does not use syllabics, a unique orthographic system of symbols that are often used to represent consonant and vowel sounds of First Nations' and Aboriginal Peoples' languages in written form. The syllabic system is used in the Cross Lake, Norway House region, however, so the reader will see the use of both roman orthography and the syllabic system in the other version of *Wild Berries: Pakwa che Menisu*, ᐸᐠᐚ ᒋ ᒥᓂᓱ.

WILD BERRIES pikaci-mīnisa *pi-ga-chi mee-ni-suh*

HIS GRANDMA ōkoma *oo-co-muh*

BEARS maskwak *mus-kwuk*

THEIR BUCKETS otaskīkowāwa *o-tus-key-co-waa-wuh*

BLUEBERRIES ininimina *i-nin-i-mi-nuh*

FOR A LONG TIME konēsk *co-nehsk*

SO MANY mīcēt *mee-cheht*

ANT ēnik *eh-nick*

SPIDER kōkom-minākēsīs *co-kom-min-naa-geh-sees*

FOX mākēsīs *maa-geh-cease*

BIRDS pinēsīsak *pi-neh-see-suck*

THEY SAY THANK YOU nanāskomowak *nuh-nass-co-moo-wuk*

WOODS sakāk *suh-gaak*

SING nikamo *ni-guh-mo*

VOWEL SOUNDS

Ā long a, *sounds like the 'a' in glad, lad*

A short a, *sounds like the 'u' in muskrat, the 'a' in Lakota, Dakota*

Ē long e, *sounds like the 'e' in the expression eh!, or the 'a' in mail*

Ī long i, *sounds like the 'e' in knee, me, key*

I short i, *sounds like the 'i' in lit, mitt*

Ō long o, *sounds like the 'o' in loon, moon, lagoon*

O short o, *sounds like the 'o' in took, look, book*

CONSONANTS

C *sounds like the 'ch' in chip, cheap, cheat*

K *sometimes pronounced like a 'g', as in get, gone*

wild blueberry jam

INGREDIENTS (MAKES ONE 8-OUNCE JAR)

4 cups of wild blueberries

1/2 cup of maple or birch syrup

1 tablespoon of lemon juice

optional

2 teaspoons of finely chopped wild mint

Combine ingredients into a saucepan and bring to a boil. Simmer ingredients and stir occasionally for 20–30 minutes until thickened. Once the jam has cooled to room temperature, pour into a sterilized glass jar and store in the fridge.

The jam will keep for a week refrigerated. There are no preservatives in this recipe.

acknowledgements *ninanāskomāwak*

I WOULD LIKE TO gratefully acknowledge Earl Cook and Jennifer Thomas for their translations — Earl for his translations and pronunciation guide for this book, *Wild Berries, Pikaci-Mīnisa,* and Jennifer for our other version of *Wild Berries, Pakwa che Menisu,* ᐸᐠᐘ ᒋ ᒥᓂᓴ.

This book is dedicated to grandmothers and their grandchildren, and to my dad, Clarence Flett, who really does like sour blueberries. To my son who always points out the most impressive spider webs and for reminding me — one more deer in the drawings; thank you. Many thanks to my sister, Leanne Flett Kruger, and friends Christine Corlett and Michelle Nahanee for their support and for their second sets of ears and eyes along the way. Thank you to Dimiter Savoff and Kallie George of Simply Read Books, and to Robin Mitchell Cranfield for her thoughtful and beautiful design and layout.

A warm and heartfelt thank you to Aboriginal Languages of Manitoba, Lorna Ingrid Brown, Rita Campbell, Laura Frisbie, Anita Large, Shannon Letandre, John McCandless, Roseann MacFadgen, Renate Preuss, Nicole Rosen, and Bob Smith — the community of friends and family who helped connect the many dots.

I would also like to acknowledge and thank The First Peoples' Cultural Council and the Aboriginal Arts Development Awards for supporting the project.